GUARDING HOLLY GRACE

BROTHERHOOD PROTECTORS WORLD

SUSAN BOLES

Twisted Page Press LLC

BROTHERHOOD PROTECTORS

ORIGINAL SERIES BY ELLE JAMES

Hot SEAL Hawaiian Nights (SEALs in Paradise)

HOLLY GRACE HILL'S sneakers pounded out a rhythm on the tar-over-gravel country road and her breath frosted the early morning December air. She supposed a lot of people wouldn't consider forty-five degrees at six in the morning to be all that cold. But to this north Mississippi gal, it was darn cold. Only her dedication to staying in shape got her out of bed on these frosty mornings to run her five-mile route before starting her day at the rescue group.

The beam of the headlamp on her head was the only light this early in the day. But she had no fear being out here alone. Not much happened in this small town. Besides, she had protection.

Grover, her rescue dog galloped at her side, totally oblivious to the fact that he was guarding her. It was a game to him. He loved to run and play. Adopting him was one of the best things she'd ever done. Who needed a boyfriend with all the baggage that came with that situation when you could have a dog that adored you every minute? Resolutely she pushed away the memories of her last relationship. No need to revisit *that* total train wreck.

One. Two. One. Two. As her feet continued to pound the pavement, she noticed the sky to the east begin to show a pink blush on the horizon. She picked up her pace to stay on schedule. Her run would be better spent thinking about her day at the rescue group instead of the past. Coordinating events for No Street For You had become her passion when she took over the position after her friend, Piper McKenzie, had moved to Montana with her Brotherhood Protectors husband.

Her steps brought her back to the edge of town just as the sun began glowing orange against the sky. The Christmas decorations that had been put up by the town council last week made cherry notes of seasonal cheer all around the town square and courthouse lawn. A massive evergreen sported bright red and white decorations and potted poinsettias graced the steps of the courthouse.

Running past the town square, she noted Ben Carter, the county sheriff, exiting his car. No doubt on his way into his office since he didn't seem to be in a hurry. He was a real workaholic. She often saw him on her early morning runs. She waved a quick greeting and continued her way.

Almost home now. Thoughts of a steaming hot shower kept her moving.

The sound of puppy yaps greeted her entrance to the small home she'd purchased last year a mile out from the town square. Despite being tired from her run, her lips turned up in a big grin at the sound and she laughed out loud when she rounded the corner into her kitchen and saw the yellow lab mix puppies pushing each other out of the way inside the crate to be the first to get her attention.

She was fostering the puppies as part of the

rescue group. As soon as she released the catch to the door, the puppies tumbled out and began attacking her feet. Grainger, the boy, got his little teeth on her shoestrings and pulled while Gracie, the girl, tried to climb up Holly Grace's calf using her sharp little puppy claws.

She reached down and gently detached both puppies clinging paws. "Now, come on you two. I have to get showered and dressed to go to the rescue meeting. The two of you need to go outside and take care of business." Delightful baby yaps met her words and the puppies wiggled and jumped trying to persuade her to get on the floor and play with them.

Do. Not. Do. It. She told herself as her knees bent, lowering her to the floor. Puppy breath and kisses greeted her as she lay full length allowing the little ones to attack her with love. She'd never been very good at listening. And she could be a little late to the meeting.

Just this once.

They'd only been playing for a few minutes when she saw Grainger squat. Letting out a yelp, she scrambled to her feet, startling both puppies. At least it caught Grangers attention and stopped him peeing on her floor. She fast walked to the back door and opened it. The puppies raced outside, across her wood deck. In their rush to get to the back yard, both puppies tumbled down the three steps to the grass. Heart in her mouth, she rushed across the deck.

Before she could get to them, both puppies stood and raced off. She watched closely but neither one showed any signs of harm and her heartbeat slowed as a grin lit her face. Was there anything in the world more adorable than puppies playing? Grover came out of the house and sat at her feet. He looked up at her and his expression clearly conveyed his own feelings about the puppies. They were taking attention away from him. She crouched and scuffed him behind his ears.

"Don't worry, Gro. The puppies are temporary, and you are forever." His tail thumped against the wooden deck and he licked her face. She glanced out into the yard and saw Grainger and Gracie rolling together in the dead grass. She called them to her, knowing they'd be covered in dead grass that would get all over the house as they raced around before she could get them back in the crate.

A frustrating ten minutes later, she had both puppies corralled back in the crate with a grinning Grover standing next to her. He'd been no help whatsoever. But was there anything in the world more precious than the unconditional love of a dog? Not like a man who promised forever and then went off to another country and got himself shot dead. *Click.* She flipped a switch on those thoughts the same way she would have turned off a light. *Nothing to see here.*

She glanced around the open living room, dining room, kitchen area and noted the expected pieces of dry grass scattered far and wide. Letting out a big sigh, she pushed her hair out of her eyes. Clean up would have to wait till this evening. The puppies yapped their displeasure from inside the wire crate as she walked away, nearly breaking her resolve to get on to work as quickly as possible.

A half hour later, she arrived at the parking lot of No Street For You Rescue group where she worked as the marketing and social media director. The title didn't really mean much since the entire team consisted of three people plus as many volunteers as they could get at any given point in time.

But she loved the organization and was grateful that Piper had recommended her as a replacement.

Holly Grace had returned to Mercy six months ago. She didn't like to think about her reasons for returning, though. So, she pushed them away as she exited her car, walked across the cold asphalt parking lot and pushed open the outer door to the building. Why was she having so much trouble with those unwanted memories today?

A blast of welcome warm air brushed against her cold cheeks, stirring the tendrils of hair curling around her face.

"Hey!" Alice Landers called. "You're late." But she softened the statement with a smile.

Holly Grace shrugged off her coat and sat at her desk, pulling her calendar to her. "The puppies caused a bit of trouble this morning."

Alice laughed. "They have a habit of doing that. But it's good that you've taken them home with you to foster. That way they get social integration and potty training. It'll make them easier to adopt out." She took a sip from the ever-present coffee cup on her desk and added. "Besides, Mollie is running late too, so no big deal with being late."

Holly Grace laughed. "Well, then. I'm not holding up our meeting if she's late too." She glanced at the photos of Grover with Gracie and Grainger she had displayed on her desk. "Those sweet puppies are worth all the trouble. They make me smile every time I see them."

"Oh! And before I forget to tell you, Piper called before you got here." Alice said, eyes dancing. "She and Ian are coming home for a few weeks."

"That's great news!" Holly Grace's mood took a big upswing. "I can't wait to see the two of them again. Where are they going to stay?"

"They're going to stay with Ian's mom." Alice answered with a tiny eyeroll. "Not much action will be going on in that house."

"Now, Alice. Don't be mean. You know Missy Elliott is great." She shrugged. "But you're probably right that not much action will take place. I think I'd be too weirded out about being in my mother-in-law's house to do anything."

Alice choked on her coffee. "Too true!" She said, wiping coffee off her chin.

"We'll have to have a girl's sleepover while she's here." Holly Grace said, then laughed. "It'll be just like old times."

"Hopefully not *too* much like old times." Alice gave her a sideways look. "We don't want Sheriff Carter catching us up to no good."

"At least he can't call our parents and rat us out these days."

Alice shook her head. "I wouldn't be too sure about that. This is such a small town I figure he'd do it just because he can."

Both laughed as Mollie came through the front door bringing a gust of cold air into the room.

"What's got you two laughing so early in the morning?" She inquired, placing a cardboard carrier with three coffees on her desk. "This is why I'm a bit late. I got held up at the Grits and Gravy. They have peppermint hot chocolate back on the menu for Christmas!"

"Yum!" Chorused Alice and Holly Grace, each of them taking a cup.

As they settled around the wobbly table they referred to as their conference table,

Mollie said, 'I heard through the grapevine that the Stewart kennels are under investigation again for suspicion of being a puppy mill."

Holly Grace gulped down a big swallow of her hot chocolate, coughed until she thought she would never breath again, and finally got herself back under control.

"Good. I hope they don't weasel out of the charges again. Maybe I should do something to help the investigation along."

Mollie shook her head. "No. Let the experts handle it." She narrowed her eyes. "I mean it, Holly Grace. Don't get involved. Those people are dangerous."

CHAPTER 2

GAGE "BOOGIE MAN" Lewis accelerated his rental car along the country road toward Mercy, Mississippi where his buddy, Ian, was spending the Christmas holidays with his wife and mother. His nickname had come from his smooth moves on the dance floor, but it wasn't unusual for people to think it referred to the mythical guy who crept up on people at night. And, Gage was content to leave it that way. That definition suited the dark mood he'd been in for months.

No point in explaining things to everyone in the world. Especially now that he wasn't in the Army anymore. The snap of a rope. A hard fall from a cliff. A lost kidney. And the loss of his ranger career.

He pressed harder on the accelerator, ignoring the warning voice in his head. The one that pointed out he didn't know this road and that dawn was several minutes away. Screw that.

He fishtailed around a sharp turn and, just like that, a woman and dog appeared in the bright beam of his headlights. Reacting immediately, he stood on the brakes and swerved the car to the left, assuming the woman and dog would run to his right since the woman's body was turned slightly in that direction.

With a sigh of relief, he saw her sprint in the direction he had predicted. Good to know his instincts were still in working order. He threw the car in reverse and maneuvered so that the headlights shone on the road. Slamming the car into park, he exited in one jump, pulling his still tender abdominal muscles.

A highly toned blonde wearing spandex pants, mittens, a puffer jacket and earmuffs glared as she strode up to him. "Are you okay?" He asked, noticing the tip of her nose was cherry red and complimented the ice blue of her eyes.

She strode right up to him, placed both palms on his chest and shoved. Surprised, he took a step back. The dog growled. Which was a bit comical as it was a pretty goofy looking dog.

"Are you out of your freaking mind?"

The woman was practically spitting in his face. And her headlamp was blinding him. He raised one hand to block the light.

"I. Uh."

"Only a fool drives like that on a road like this." Her eyes raked over him. "And I don't recognize you which means you're not local. So, in addition to this being a curvy road in the dark, you've never driven on it before." The dog growled again, and she put a hand on its head. It stopped growling but kept its eyes on him.

"You're right." He said. "I was driving pretty irresponsibly. I didn't think there would be anyone out here at this hour." He saw he draw breath. No doubt for a further tirade. "And that's no excuse. I know that."

"Who are you and what are you doing out here?"

"I'm Gage Lewis. I'm on my way to a town called Mercy to spend the holiday with my buddy, Ian Elliott."

That seemed to take the wind out of her sails just a bit, so he pushed his luck. "Do you think you could turn off the headlamp? I feel like I'm in a really bad movie being given the third degree."

She frowned but reached up and switched the light off. He lowered his hand far enough to reach out to her. "I'd like to introduce myself properly. Gage Lewis. I work for the Brotherhood Protectors and I'm friends with Ian Elliott and his wife Piper. I'm here for the holidays."

Slowly she reached out and took his hand, still watching him with wary eyes. "Holly Grace Hill. Friend of Ian and Piper all my life."

"What are you doing way out here in the dark." He inquired, releasing her hand.

"I'm running. I run every morning. This is my regular route." She stepped back from him, her hand on the dog's head. "And, before today, I've never been almost run down by a car."

Ouch. She had a point. He'd let his mood make him careless. "I'm truly sorry about that. Can I give you a lift home?"

She gave him an incredulous look from those icy eyes. "Absolutely not. I'm not inclined to get in a car with you for any reason."

A year ago, before his accident, he would have considered her a challenge, but at this point, he didn't have the inclination to chase a pretty woman. He was too busy getting his feet back under him with the Brotherhood Protectors and coming to grips with the lose of his army ranger career. So, he nodded and accepted her verdict.

"Okay. I guess if you're friends with Ian and Piper, I'll see you around town while I'm here."

She quirked an eyebrow, reached up and turned her headlamp back on and said, "I assume you know how to get to Miz Elliott's house?"

He nodded. She motioned to the dog and the two of them went along the road in the direction he'd been headed before he'd almost run her down.

He let out a breath he hadn't realized he'd been holding and ran a hand through his hair.

This could have been very bad. He had to get a grip on himself. Killing one or crippling someone wasn't something he wanted to be party to.

He got back into the rental, pulled onto the road and proceeded at a much more reasonable speed. When his headlights picked the girl and dog out of the dark, she moved all the way into the knee-high weeds, getting as far off the road as she could. And keeping the dog between herself and the fence next to her.

He slowed the car even more. As he came even with her, he glanced over. She looked back, nodded and then looked front again. He touched the horn just enough to make a quiet honk, sped up a bit and proceeded into town.

As he rolled into the town square, he saw an older man in a uniform walk across the courthouse lawn and enter the building. People sure started work early here. As he contemplated who the man might be, his cell phone rang. Glancing over to it, lying on the passenger seat, he saw it was Ian.

He pressed the accept phone call button on the steering wheel. "Hey, dude."

"Hey." Ian responded over the speaker. "Are you close?"

"Yep. I'm in the town square."

"Okay. Go around the square, then take the road next to It'll Grow Back salon and go five miles. We're on the right. Red brick house, double garage. I'll leave the porch light on."

"It'll Grow Back?" Gage asked.

"Yeah. It's the local beauty shop. Where all the ladies gather to discuss everyone and everything in town. Welcome to a small town in the south. I'll introduce you around once you've gotten some rest."

"I actually already met someone." Gage said, cruising the town square until he spotted the beauty shop sign and proceeding down the road next to it as Ian had advised.

"You did?" Ian questioned.

"Yeah. She said she knows you and Piper."

"She?"

"Yep."

Ian groaned. "Was it, Holly Grace?"

"Yes." He responded and went on to explain the circumstances.

In the background, he heard a woman's voice. Ian replied. "I'm talking to him now. He almost ran down Holly Grace and Grover out on the county road."

As he heard Piper's raised voice in the background, he couldn't help but wonder if he would be the main topic of conversation at the It'll Grow Back for the duration of his stay.

CHAPTER 3

"Y'ALL ARE NOT GOING to believe what happened on my run this morning." Holly Grace said as she entered the rescue group office. Mollie and Alice looked up from their desks, eyebrows raised.

She hung her coat on a hook by the front door, sat at her desk and popped her purse into the bottom drawer.

"Well, spill!" Alice exclaimed. "Don't leave us hanging."

She described the events of her early morning job to her friends. Whose eyes got bigger and bigger as her story progressed.

Mollie grunted. "Talk about irresponsible! And you say he works with this protection group with Ian? Not very good at it, is he? I'm glad you and Grover are both okay."

"Was he good looking?" Alice asked.

Holly Grace frowned. "What's that got to do with anything?"

"Ha!" Alice clapped her hands. "He is."

"I didn't say that." Holly Grace protested.

"Right. You avoided answering which means you *do* think he's good looking."

"Oh, for crying out loud." Holly Grace said.

"Look. You need to get your toes back in the dating water."

Holly Grace opened her mouth to protest, but Alice held up her hand.

"Hear me out." She said. "Colt is gone. It's awful that he got shot in Afghanistan. And I understand your grief. Y'all dated since you were fifteen. But, it's time to get back out there. And who better than someone who's only going to be in town for a short time? He'll be gone back to wherever they live in the protection group and you'll have gotten started back on the land of the living."

Mollie nodded in agreement.

Before Holly Grace could reply to such an outrageous suggestion, her phone rang. Thank goodness. "No Street For You rescue. Holly Grace speaking."

Avoiding the eyes of her friends, she took down the information from the caller about a stray dog wander the woods on the edge of town.

"I'll head right out there and take a look." She told the caller. "Thank you for letting us know."

She hung up, cut her eyes to the side and saw both other women busy at their own desks.

"I'm heading out to take a look for a young shepherd mix out on the north side of town."

"Do you need one or both of us to go with you?" Mollie asked.

Holly Grace shrugged back into her coat. "I don't think so. But when I get out there if it looks like a more than one-person job, I'll call y'all."

Driving her Honda Civic around the town square to the road north, she went back over Alice's words about dating. She knew her friends had her best interests at heart, but she wasn't certain she was ready to let go of Colt. He'd been an integral part of her life. Her first boyfriend. All her firsts. Kiss, sex, husband. How could she even think of building a relationship with someone else?

She made a quick stop at the Grits and Gravy for two sausage biscuits to help lure the dog to her.

Back in her car, she slowed to a crawl as she took the north road out of town, eyes scanning the roadside for the shepherd mix. She went three miles along the road without seeing the dog. Making a three-point turn, she headed back toward town, scanning the opposite side of the road. Maybe she should have brought Alice or Mollie with her. It was impossible to scan both sides of the road while driving and she worried she was moving right past the poor dog without seeing it.

As the town square came back into view, she decided. She'd have to look on foot. This just was not working. She pulled her car to the side of the road, got out and took her hiking boots from the trunk. As she laced them onto her feet, a black Nissan Altima cruised in her direction. Not recognizing the car, she looked away, scanning the roadside immediately around her for signs of the dog.

The car pulled up next to her and the window lowered. She glanced over, prepared to nod in acknowledgement of whoever it might be. But that didn't happen. Instead, she frowned.

"You."

The man who'd nearly mowed her down this morning, gave her a sheepish look. What was his name again? Ugh. She couldn't remember.

He had the grace to look embarrassed. "I guess I'm the last person you want around. But I saw you out here by yourself and thought maybe you are stranded or need help."

Pointedly, she looked back to the town square a quarter mile behind him. "I'm fine. I got a call about a stray dog that needs rescuing and I'm out her looking for it."

"Alone?"

She sighed. "Yes. Alone. It's not likely that anything will happen to me. And if the dog turns out to be more than I can handle, I'll call one of my coworkers to come out and help me with the rescue."

"I'll help you." He offered. "I feel like I owe

you after what happened earlier this morning. Gage Lewis to the rescue."

Thank goodness. Now she knew his name. She put her hands on her hips. "You don't owe me anything other than your word that you'll be more careful in the future. Besides, you're not trained for this."

He glanced around, looked her over, and said, "I don't think it's all that complicated, right? I mean we're just going to get the dog into your car, and you'll take it to your shelter. Correct?"

She threw her hands in the air. "Fine. Park your car while I get my gear out of mine."

She took two rope leashes with no ring on them from the car. They didn't have a buckle on them. Instead the rope threaded back through an opening in the rope itself so that it adjusted to the size of the dog's neck. Very handy for getting a leash on a skittish dog without getting your hands close to their mouth. She grabbed the white paper bag with two sausage biscuits in it she'd bought earlier, then, she opened the door of the medium size crate that was crammed in her back seat. A Civic didn't have a lot of room for a crate and she hoped the dog was as young, and the size, that the caller had told her.

She glanced up at the sound of footsteps. He was back. And, fortunately, wearing boots that would stand up to hiking.

She handed him one of the leashes and a wrapped sausage biscuit. "If you see the dog, be very calm. Very slow. And speak gently. Persuade it that you are its friend and will help it. If you can get close to the dog, put this around its neck." She hesitated. "Actually, if you see the dog, just signal me. I'll take it from there."

He took the leash from her hand. "No worries. I can handle this."

"You don't have to help me. I'm perfectly fine on my own. I don't need anyone to look out for me."

His eyes met hers. His reflected concern. She couldn't imagine what hers might be reflecting. She admitted to herself that he was far too good looking and she wasn't sure she wanted to feel that magnetism. It might be best to send him on his way before something started that she didn't feel ready to deal with just yet.

"I'm happy to help out. I promise I won't screw anything up this time."

She pulled her eyes away from his gaze. "Well. Okay. I do need some help spotting the dog. It seems to be pretty good at hiding."

They took opposite sides of the road and began walking softly along. Holly Grace kept her eyes on the task at hand, hoping she'd spot the dog quickly.

Thirty minutes later, she sensed more than saw a slight movement in the underbrush. She stood perfectly still to see if the movement repeated. Gage must have been watching her, because she didn't hear him walking in the dry grass behind her.

A tiny breeze stirred her hair. Seconds ticked by. Then minutes. She stayed perfectly still. At last, a small movement proved she'd been right. Now that she knew the exact place to look, she could discern the dog's brown and black coloring among the dead brush it was hiding in.

Holly Grace tucked the leash into the back of her jeans to leave her hands free. She didn't want to frighten the dog. Both hands extended and open, she stepped slowly in the direction of the dog. She could see the dog's eyes now. They watched her warily, but it didn't make a move away from her. Good. In a soft voice she spoke to it.

"That's right. I'm your friend. I'm going to get you to a warm, safe place with plenty of food."

She hoped Gage wouldn't try to come closer. She worried he might scare the dog into running away. She listened for a moment but didn't hear any sounds. Maybe he had some common sense after all.

The dog stood, turned its head as though it might bolt. She stopped. "Look." She said, I have a biscuit here. It's for you. Will you take it?"

The dog looked at the bag in her hands. She removed the sausage biscuit, pinched off a piece of it and tossed it gently toward the dog. She could see its nose twitching as it caught the scent of food. It looked back to her, then at the food. It took one tentative step toward the biscuit piece. When she didn't make any moves herself, it took another step, then grabbed the food.

It took another half hour before she was

able to lure the dog to her and get the leash on its neck. Once that step was accomplished, the dog let her pick it up and carry it to her car and put it in the crate. She crooned sweet nothings to the dog the entire time and tried to avoid looking at Gage who followed her very closely and, in a very soft voice so as not to frighten the dog, suggested she let him do the carrying in case the dog went crazy.

She ignored him.

Once the dog was secured in the crate in her car, she took the second sausage biscuit from Gage and poked it through the wire door of the crate.

"All's well that ends well." She told Gage, taking the extra leash from him and tossing it in the floorboard with the leash she had removed from the dog when she put it in the crate.

"That was amazing." He told her with a sincere look in his eyes.

She felt a flush crawling up her cheeks and bent over to unlace her hiking boots so that he wouldn't see.

"It's usually not hard. You just have to have a lot of patience and understanding." She said from her bent over position. She slipped off the hiking boots and snagged her sneakers from the car. After she switched out her shoes there was no excuse not to stand up and look at him.

He held out his hand. She took it. And sparks flew.

CHAPTER 4

GAGE FELT as though he'd grabbed onto an electric fence the moment his hand connected with Holly Grace's. They'd shook hands last night and nothing remotely like this had happened. So, what had changed? He didn't know and wasn't sure he liked it. There were too many variables in his life right now to add romance to the mix.

Holly Grace looked as stunned as he felt, and they hastily released each other's hand.

"Well." Holly Grace said. "I better get this baby to the rescue office so we can get her ready to go to the vet for a thorough work up before we figure out if she can go into a foster home."

"Uh. Right." He said. *Real smooth, man.* Could he be any more awkward? "I guess I'll see you around, then."

Holly Grace nodded, then got into her car and drove off. He stood in the road where she'd left him watching her go.

Gage got into his own car and drove into the town square. He'd told Ian and Piper and Ian's mom he'd get breakfast for them from some place there called Grits and Gravy that was apparently their favorite place to eat. He'd gotten distracted when he'd spotted Holly Grace leaving heading out of town and been curious enough to stop and involve himself in her rescue. Now he suspected that the Elliott's might be wondering what had happened to their breakfast. Looking at the dash clock on his rental he realized he'd been gone almost an hour.

Damn. This was going to take some explaining on his part. He picked up his cellphone from the cup holder and saw that he'd missed two calls from Ian. Might as well face the music now.

Ian picked up as soon as the call connected. "Hey, man. Where are you?"

Gage sighed. "I got distracted. I'm heading to the café now and will be there with breakfast as fast as they can cook it and bag it up for me."

"So, what have you been doing instead of getting breakfast?" Ian wondered.

"I ran into Holly Grace trying to capture a stray and stayed to help her."

"You don't say."

"Well, the ladies will no doubt forgive you for helping a damsel, but I'm starving, so you better get some food and get on back here."

"It's not like that." Gage grumbled. "And hold your horses. I'll be there with the food pronto."

A parking spot opened right in front of the café as he drove up. Finally, a bit of good luck. Inside, he found a huge Christmas tree right by the counter holding the cash register. It nearly reached the ceiling and was absolutely covered in Christmas ornaments of every shape, size and color. Multi-colored blinking lights ran around the room at the ceiling casting pretty colors along the walls. A short, older woman with a braid that reached to her waist met him at the register. Her name tag said Helen.

"What can I do for you, Hon?" She asked him, taking a pen from behind her ear and an order pad from the back pocket of her jeans. "Don't believe I've seen you around here before."

"No." He answered. "This is my first time in town. I'm visiting Ian and Piper Elliott."

Her eyes gave him the once over. "You work with Ian at that protector place out in Montana?"

He'd heard about the small-town phenomena of everyone knowing everyone else's business, but this was his first experience with it. It seemed a bit creepy to him. But being from a big city environment made him suspicious of everyone.

"Yes. I do work with Ian. He invited me to spend the Christmas holidays with him and Piper here."

"I guess you're all right then. Any friend of Ian and Piper is a friend of mine. What'll you have?"

He gave her the order and waited. It didn't take long before Helen was back with everything bagged up for him. "Tell Missy Elliott I'll see her tomorrow for breakfast." She said as she handed him the white paper bags.

"You'll see her tomorrow?" He questioned.

Helen laughed. "On my, yes. Missy and several other ladies here in town meet for breakfast here every Thursday. Right over there at the big center table." She grinned at him. "You might say it's the second-best place in town to get all the gossip. Next to the It'll Grow Back, of course."

"Of course." He echoed, taking the bags and exiting as quickly as was polite.

CHAPTER 5

ONCE SHE ARRIVED BACK at the rescue office, Holly Grace struggled to get the crate containing the shepherd mix out the backseat of her Civic. She didn't want to cuss, or make any loud noises, or gestures, for fear of scaring the dog. But dad gummit! This was a mess. The crate was really wedged in there.

The sweet shepherd's anxious eyes cut her to the heart. "It's okay, sweetie. I'm going to leave you out here by yourself just for a few minutes, okay?" The dog's ears twitched, but otherwise she seemed okay. Holly Grace gently closed the car door, cutting of the chilly wind blowing across the parking lot and straight into the car.

She entered the office and found both Alice and Mollie at their desks. "I got the dog. A sweet female shepherd mix. She seems okay. Just skinny and skittish."

"No trouble coaxing her to come to you?" Alice asked. "We kept expecting the phone to ring and you to ask for assistance."

Holly Grace shifted from foot to foot, reluctant to confess that Gage Lewis had helped her with the dog. After that electric shock when their hands met, she wasn't sure what to think and didn't want to discuss it with her friends until she'd digested it herself. On the other hand, she hated lying. "As a matter of fact, Ian and Piper's friend happened to come by and helped me with the capture."

The others looked at each other, then back at her.

"Really." Alice said in a smooth voice. "Wasn't that quite the coincidence."

This was exactly why she hadn't wanted to admit that Gage had helped her. She could see from the expression on Alice's face that she was mentally making a much bigger deal out of the meeting than it had been.

"I need to get the dog into the system and

ready for fostering." Holly Grace said to change the subject.

The others looked around.

"Where is she?" Asked Mollie.

"I can't get the crate out of the car." Holly Grace confessed. "It's wedged in tight. I thought I'd come on in and call the vet to see if I can bring her over there for a once over instead of getting her out and then back into the car."

Mollie nodded. "Good idea." She reached for the phone on her desk, dialed and listened. After confirming with their vet that they could take the dog now, Mollie hung up and nodded to Holly Grace. "They said bring her on in."

"Great!" Holly Grace turned to go back outside.

"Wait." Mollie called.

She turned; eyebrows raised. "I heard something that I wanted to talk to you about."

Holly Grace moved to the chair next to Mollie's desk and sat. "Yes?"

Mollie gave her a once over. "Remember I told you that kennel you hate is being investigated again?"

She nodded.

"I heard this morning that someone had called in an anonymous tip that got the investigation started."

Holly Grace remained still.

"Were you the one that called it in?"

Holly Grace noticed Alice pretending not to be listening, but her ears were all but flapping.

"What if I was?" Holly Grace asked. "Those people are running a puppy mill out there and need to be stopped."

Mollie sighed. "I had a feeling it was you. That was a dangerous thing to do, Holly Grace. Those people make a lot of money off their operation and are furious that they're under investigation again. If they find out it was you that got it started, they might do something in retaliation."

Holly Grace crossed her arms over her chest. "I don't care. They need to be stopped. And, since there is an investigation going on, I don't believe they'll do something so risky as retaliating against me. And that's assuming they find out it was me. It was an anonymous tip."

Mollie shook her head. "You are such an innocent sometimes, Holly Grace. People have a way of finding out things in small towns like this. You know that."

"I do know that." She agreed. "And I'll be careful. But I'm not sorry I did it."

She stood to go out to the dog. It must be getting anxious by now. She hadn't intended to be inside this long.

"I'm going to take the dog to the vet, then head over to the town square to help finish up things for the big tree lighting and party at the train depot tonight. Are y'all going to be there?"

Both women agreed that they would see her there.

CHAPTER 6

"So. Holly Grace, huh?" Ian said.

Gage ignored him, not yet ready to discuss anything to do with the lovely lady. He hadn't yet digested his own reactions and feelings.

"For heaven's sake, Ian. Leave him alone." Piper Elliott said, swatting her husband on the arm. "Can't you see he doesn't want to talk about her?"

While grateful for Piper's defense, Gage wondered if she saw him too clearly for his own comfort.

"What's on the agenda today?" He asked. "Are you two going to give me the fifty-cent tour of your hometown?"

"The Christmas Committee could probably

use some help getting the tree ready for lighting and the train depot ready for the party." Ian's mother said from her place at the kitchen table where she was finishing off the breakfast Gage had brought from the Grits and Gravy café.

Ian turned to look at her. "That's tonight?"

His mother nodded.

He turned to Gage with a huge grin on his face. "Man, you are in for a treat if you really want to get an up-close look at small town life."

"Is Miss Edna still running the show?" Piper asked her mother-in-law who nodded.

She gave Gage a delighted look. "Miss Edna is a not to be missed phenomena in the town of Mercy."

"Why do I feel like I'm being set up?" Gage asked all three of them.

"No set up." Ian commented. "Just some real small-town celebrations."

"You kids go on to the town square and help out." Ian's mother pushed them all toward the door, grabbing coats as she went.

"Why don't you come with us, Mama? They may want you to help, too."

Missy Elliott smiled. "No, I won't come

with y'all. I want the three of you to have a good time together. Lily Gayle Lambert is coming by to pick me up later."

Ian and Piper snickered as the went out to Ian's truck.

"What's so funny?" Gage asked, opening the passenger door the truck and motioning Piper ahead of him.

"Lily Gayle Lambert is another one of our town phenoms." Piper told him as she slid to the into the passenger seat.

He waited until he'd buckled himself into the back seat before asking. "Is this town full of unusual people?"

Ian backed the truck out onto the road and headed toward town. "I guess all small towns have their share of eccentrics, but we feel we have the most original. Miss Edna must be in her eighties by now and she's the stereotypical town busybody. She has a home on the square. One of those old Victorian monstrosities. She sits on the porch regularly with her bird watching binoculars."

"Let me guess." Gage said. "She's watching people instead of birds."

"Got it in one." Piper replied. "And Lily Gayle Lambert is younger than Miss Edna. She's Ian's mom's age, but she's a busy body in her own way. She butt's into Sheriff Carter's cases all the time. It drives him nuts."

"Why doesn't he just make her butt out?" Gage asked, wondering how all these women got away with this stuff. Not that he had anything against independent thinking and acting women. But if he had two that were borderline breaking the law, he believed he's put the brakes to those activities.

"She's the sheriff's first cousin. And they're the only ones left from their family." Ian said. "So, I guess poor Ben Carter just puts up with her. Besides, no one has ever been able to tell Miss Lily Gayle what to do a day in her life, and it's probably too late to start now."

"You have to give her credit though. She did solve the wolfman murder. And the murder during the sleep study up at the Midnight Dragonfly." Piper added, turning to shoot a wicked grin at Gage.

"Now you're pulling my leg." Gage said. "There's no such thing as a wolfman."

"There sure is. And it was the talk of the county, and for miles around when it happened." Piper insisted.

Ian eased the big truck into a parking space on the town square and the three of them exited. Half the town must be milling around helping with lights on the huge tree on the lawn of the courthouse. Decorations already covered the tree from top to bottom, so Gage hoped that the lights had already been put on it. Otherwise it would be an incredibly difficult job to get them arranged around all those ornaments.

"Look!" Piper pointed off to their left. "That's the old train depot where we have our annual town Christmas party. Be careful on the punch though. Miss Edna's secret ingredient is moonshine."

Before he could inquire further about the source of the moonshine for the punch, Piper waved vigorously at someone.

"Hey, Holly Grace!" Piper called.

Gage was careful to keep a neutral expression on his face, but there was nothing he could do about his heart racing unexpectedly in his chest. If someone had bet him he'd fall for a girl the day after nearly running her down on a country road, he'd have told them they were out of their mind.

His racing heart told him it was a bet he'd have lost.

CHAPTER 7

Holly Grace turned to find the person shouting her name. It sounded like Piper Elliott. Sure enough, when she scanned the courthouse lawn, there was Piper, along with Ian. And Gage Lewis.

She tried to tell herself that seeing Piper again after all these months was the sole reason for her sudden surge of happiness. Her brain wasn't buying that though. Somehow, she'd managed to fall for the infuriating Gage.

How could this have happened? Another military man when she'd sworn never to give her heart to one again. Her heart tried to tell her he was no longer in the military if he worked with Ian, so there was that. But her brain kicked in and mentioned that the agency Ian worked for made their money protecting people. Hence the name Brotherhood Protectors. And protectors got shot at sometimes.

Ignoring the internal argument, her feet led her right over to the threesome.

Piper engulfed her in a tight hug. "Girl! I've missed you so much! How's everything going?"

"Great! I'm loving my job at the rescue group. I'm fostering two lab mix puppies."

"How's Grover taking that?"

Holly Grace frowned. "He's not crazy about it, but he's just being distant with them. Not aggressive at all."

"Any romantic interests?" Piper inquired with an innocent look on her face.

Holly Grace concentrated to keep a blush from staining her cheeks. Of course, Piper had an innocent look in her face. She had no idea that Holly Grace had discovered feeling for the visitor. She carefully did not look in Gage's direction, but sensed he was waiting to hear her answer. Could it be possible he had feelings for her as well? The thought that he might caused an upsurge of excitement inside her. Stop it, she told herself. Don't read something into the situation that isn't there. He's just paying attention because he has nice manners.

"Uh. No." She answered Piper's question. "Nothing going on in that department."

Was that a glint in Gage's eyes? Was he glad to hear her say there was no one?

"Come on, Piper." Ian said, breaking into Holly Grace's thoughts. "Leave her be." He grinned at Holly Grace. "I want to hear more about how you were going to kick Gage's butt out on the county road yesterday."

A blush she couldn't control this time crept up her cheeks. "It was just adrenaline. Y'all know. Fight or flight. Somebody almost ran me down, so I pushed back."

"As well you should have." Gage replied, coming to her rescue. "I had no business driving that fast on any road. Much less one I'd never driven on before."

Before Holly Grace could think of a reply, someone shouted in the distance.

"Piper! Ian! Y'all get on over here and hug my neck. I can't believe y'all didn't let me know you're in town."

Holly Grace glanced at Gage as Piper and

Ian, holding hands, strolled over to greet their old friend.

"Soooo. Are you enjoying your visit to Mercy?"

Gage's lips curved into a smile. "I came out with Ian and Piper to get some experience of Christmas in a small southern town. I was assured that there are some local characters that I should meet."

Holly Grace quirked an eyebrow. "Which ones did you hear about? We have a town full of characters."

"One is named Miss Edna. I was told she not only is she informed about most people's business but that she is also the maker of the Christmas punch for the party tonight. And that the secret ingredient is moonshine."

Holly Grace burst into laughter. "Oh my! Piper and Ian were certainly shooting the moon with that one. Miss Edna is notorious."

Excited chatter in the direction of the courthouse caught her attention.

"And, you'll get a bird's eye view of her in just a minute. It looks like they're about ready to light the Christmas tree and Miss Edna is pulling the switch this year."

Gage held his hand out to her. "In that case, let's get a ringside view. I'd hate to miss anything."

As their hands connected, Holly Grace felt the sizzle all the way to her toes. Gage's fingers tightened on hers and she wondered if he felt it too.

They strolled through the crowd, right up to the front so that they had the ringside view Gage had wanted.

Miss Edna moved to the platform where the switch had been set up for the celebratory first lighting of the tree. One of the younger men made the mistake of trying to help her up the single step to the platform.

Miss Edna jerked her arm away from the grasp of a young man who looked to be in high school. "I don't need any assistance. I'm not ready for my grave just yet, young man. Now get out of my way. I have some important business to take care of."

The feisty old woman tottered to the switch and held up her hands for silence. The chatter gradually subsided with some shushing assistance from the crowd.

"Before I light this tree, I want to remind

everyone that we're going straight over to the train depot for the part as soon as I do this." Miss Edna said in a surprisingly strong voice for such an old woman. "And I want everyone to know that I made plenty of my Christmas punch, so we won't run out before the party's over."

A roar went up from the crowd.

Gage leaned close and whispered in her ear. "She's definitely a feisty gal. I guess they grow them that way in this town."

Holly Grace hid a giggle behind her hand. It wouldn't do for Miss Edna to see her laughing and take offense.

"And now," Miss Edna yelled. "Merry Christmas, everyone!" She flipped the switch and the thirty-foot-tall evergreen immediately glowed with twinkle lights in multiple color

The old woman tottered to the edge of the platform, stepped down and moved in the direction of the train depot with the crowd following behind. For all the world like an aged pied piper.

Holly Grace sighed, then felt Gage's eyes on her. She looked up into his face.

"You love this, don't you?" He asked, using

his free hand to trace her cheekbone with his fingers.

She shivered. Not from cold, but from the gentle touch of his hand on her face.

"Yes." She answered, not sure if she meant the tree or his hand touching her. And not sure she cared which way he took her answer.

His fingers slipped beneath her chin, tilting her face toward him. He leaned in and then hesitated as though waiting to see if she would pull away. She half closed her eyes, and within a moment his lips met hers in a gently exploratory kiss. She felt it all the way through her body. The rightness of it. She took a small step closer to him and he released the hand he had still been holding and circled his arm around her waist pulling her closer as he deepened the kiss.

Her arms slid up around his neck, tangling in his hair as she pulled his face closer to better enjoy the moment. Just as she rose to her tiptoes, a flash went off close by.

She and Gage broke apart like a couple of teenagers who'd been sneaking around. Holly Grace whirled around to find Piper hold her cellphone in position to snap another picture.

"Not funny, Piper." She said.

"Come on, you two." Piper answered. "Ian's waiting for us at the train depot. We have to make sure Gage gets some of Miss Edna's famous Christmas punch."

CHAPTER 8

THE NEXT MORNING Gage woke with a headache strikingly like the ones he'd had in his party days in college. Miss Edna's punch had definitely been potent. When he focused past the pain, he realized he had a feeling of contentment he hadn't experienced since before his accident. And he knew the source of it. Holly Grace. A Christmas miracle indeed

Rising from the bed he went to shower and hopefully shake off the effects of his overindulgence. First order of today was to find a nice florist in town where he could purchase flowers for Holly Grace and get directions to the office of the rescue group where she worked. She'd told him last night that she was working today.

An hour later he pulled his rental into the parking lot for No Street For You. Not fancy, he thought to himself as he exited the car. But Holly Grace had told him they were one hundred percent donation supported. In a small town like this it was probably hard to raise funds.

Anticipation bubbled through him as he pulled open the door. However, the bubbles burst quickly when he scanned the room and saw two women that he remembered meeting briefly last night. But no Holly Grace.

His face must have told the story because the one he thought was called Mollie said, "Holly Grace is out on a rescue. A call came in a little while ago and she took off to handle it."

Gage set the flowers on an empty desk noticing a picture of a big fuzzy dog and two small puppies. He remembered the fuzzy dog had been with Holly Grace the day she was running. This must be her desk.

"Do you know which direction she went?" He asked the woman he thought was named Mollie. "Maybe I can help her again."

Mollie and the other woman glanced at each other. He gave them credit for not smiling.

"I believe she's out on the same road where you helped her last time." Mollie replied.

"Thank you." He said and beat a hasty retreat knowing a lot of speculation would be done as soon as he was out of sight. He didn't care. He only wanted to be with Holly Grace.

He spotted Holly Grace's Civic parked almost in the same spot as last time they'd been here on a rescue. The problem was, there was no sign of Holly Grace. He parked close to her car, got out and scanned the area.

Nothing moved other than tall weeds in the wind.

"Holly Grace!" He shouted. Nothing.

"Holly Grace!" He shouted again, straining his ears to hear any sound above the wind. Nothing.

The short hairs on the nape of his neck stood up. The way they had when he was a ranger in the army and something not quite right was going on. Hoping, for the first time in his life, his instinct was wrong, he went into ranger mode.

Holly Grace's keys and purse were in the car. The ground around the car didn't appear to scuffed up. He scanned in widening circles around the car looking for anything out of the ordinary. Not until he was fifteen feet from the car, in an adjoining field, did he find something that made his blood run cold.

The dry grass was flattened, scuff marks disturbed the dirt patches in between clumps of grass, and, worst of all, drops of blood marred the ground in one small area. He touched them lightly. They were still wet. So recent. His worst fears came to the surface.

Hurrying back to his car, he used his cellphone to alert Ian that Holly Grace was missing and his fears that she had somehow come to harm. Ian informed him that the local search and rescue group would be alerted and to meet them at the train depot. The same place where he and Holly Grace had been so happy just last night.

Since he was practically at the train depot when he called Ian, Gage was the first to arrive. In short order six other men arrived, including the sheriff. Gage briefed everyone on what he knew, then turned everything over to the sheriff. As much as he wanted to run this show, he didn't want to step on anyone's toes. He'd give the sheriff a chance to prove how good he was, and, if he didn't meet Gage's standards, then he'd go off on his own. There was no way he was going to lose Holly Grace so soon after he'd found her.

Sheriff Carter contacted Mollie and Alice at the rescue office, but they had not information beyond what they'd already told Gage. Trying not to grind his teeth together at what he considered wasted time, Gage glanced at Ian to see how he was handling having the sheriff in charge instead of them. Ian gave a tiny eye roll, but no other indication.

The sheriff sent them all out to the field where Gage had found the evidence of a struggle with instruction for them to fan out in a circle looking for additional evidence that might lead them to answers about Holly Grace.

CHAPTER 9

HOLLY GRACE TRIED TO COUGH, but discovered she was gagged. When she tried to reach up and remove the gag, she discovered her hands were tied behind her back. Then that her ankles were also tied together. Just like a prize calf, she thought to herself.

The room where she was being held had one small window high on the wall, a cold concrete floor and smelled strongly of urine. And, in that moment, she knew exactly where she was and why.

Temper flaring, she determined that she would get out of this room and make very sure that the Summerall Kennel was closed down for good.

The Summerall clan had miscalculated when they grabbed her. And, also, when they tied her up. In addition to running daily, she also practiced yoga regularly. And was very flexible.

Concentrating carefully, she managed to maneuver her bound hands in front of her by pulling her bent legs close to her chest and sliding her hands beneath her feet.

Good. She told herself. Step one accomplished.

Even though her hands were still bound, she could pull the gag from her mouth. Having that nasty rag away from her tongue felt wonderful. And, with the gag gone, she could use her teeth to work at the binding on her wrists. The rope was rough, scratchy and not easily loosened. Frustration brought tears to her eyes. She considered screaming for help but knew that doing that would only make her situation worse because most likely the only one who would hear her was a member of the family holding her captive.

Best to keep quiet and extend her chance of getting herself out of this mess despite her current frustration. Taking a few moments to meditate and focus brought her determination back. She could do this.

At last, and without chipping a tooth, she managed to loosen the rope enough to slide her hands out of the binding. It was the work of a moment to get the rope off her ankles. She stood, stretched and contemplated her next step.

The only window didn't have a latch to open it. Firmly cemented on all four sides and webbed with wire, she knew it would be a waste of time to try and knock it out. There was one door to the cinderblock room, and she knew before she tried the knob that it would be locked.

She twisted it anyway. Because what else did she have to do right this minute? Yep. Locked tight.

With a sigh, she contemplated the situation. She had nothing but the clothes on her back. No handy lock pick or cellphone. Her smart watch had been removed. No doubt to keep her from using it to summon help. But she also had no way of determining the time and now long she'd been gone. Surely Mollie and Alice would sound an alarm if she'd been gone an unusually long time.

Defeated for the moment, she slid down the wall opposite the door until her butt sat firmly on the cold floor. There had to be something she could do to get out of here. No telling when one of the Summerall's might show up and discover her untied.

CHAPTER 10

"Come on, man." Gage said to Ian. "This is getting us nowhere."

Ian glanced around to see who might be within hearing distance. "This is what the sheriff wants to do, so we're doing it. Neither one of us is in charge here."

Gage blew out a frustrated breath and ran a hand through his hair. "Seriously? If it was Piper would you be going along with this?"

Ian didn't respond.

"I knew it." Gage said. "You wouldn't be doing this if it was Piper. Well, I'm not going along with this on Holly Grace either. Do you know the number to the rescue group? I want to talk to those ladies. Find out if anything weird has been going on lately."

Ian gave him a doubtful look. "You think her disappearing has something to do with the dog rescue?"

"It's the best place we've got to start at this point. Let's talk to those ladies and see if anything turns up."

They edged away from the others working the grid of the field, fading into the woods nearby and working their way back to Ian's truck. "Come on." Ian said. "Let's just take my truck and go over there and see what they have to say."

Gage's answer was to jump in the passenger seat and buckle up. "Let's go. Time's wasting."

Mollie and Alice latched on to them the minute they walked in the door wanting to know what was going on and any progress being made in finding Holly Grace.

"Look." Gage said. "The local men are out there scouring the field where I found the scuff marks and blood but aren't turning up anything yet. I wanted to come in here and talk to the two of you. Is there anything, I mean anything, unusual that happened lately? Even something that may seem unrelated."

The two women gave him frightened looks. "I don't know what to tell you." Alice responded. "I swear there's nothing I can think of that could possibly relate to her disappearing like this." Tear swam in her eyes and Gage felt sorry for her. She was obviously distraught over her friend's disappearance.

"What about you?" He questioned Mollie. "Is there anything you can think of?"

Mollie looked uncertain. He knew she was thinking something over. Something that might lead them to Holly Grace.

"I can see you have something on your mind, Mollie. Why don't you tell us so that we can make a decision about how it might be related to this?"

Mollie put her head in her hands. "I told her she'd made a mistake. I told her."

Gage sat in the chair next to her desk. Took her hand in his. "Please. I know you care about her. I know you don't want anything to happen to her. Please tell me what you're thinking."

"The Summerall's." Mollie said.

Ian hissed.

Mollie glanced in his direction. "Yes. The kennel. I found out the other day that Holly Grace had called in an anonymous report about them running a puppy mill."

"And you think they know it was Holly Grace who called it in?"

Mollie frowned. "You obviously don't come from a small town. I don't care how anonymous you think something is. When you live where everybody knows everybody and all their business, for generations back, there is no anonymity."

Gage looked to Ian who nodded. "She's right. What was Holly Grace thinking to do something like that?"

"How do we get there?" Gage asked, heading for the door.

"Hold up." Ian said. "We have no evidence that the Summerall's are involved in Holly Grace's disappearance."

Gage continued to the door. "We don't have any other clues. I'm going to follow this one. If it doesn't pan out, I'll find another one. And another one. Until we find her."

Ian followed him out the door. "Okay. Okay. Get in the truck. It can't hurt to drive out there and ask if they've seen her. Maybe sniff around a bit just in case."

Ian turned his truck off the country road fifteen minutes out from town.

At first Gage didn't see anything. Just woods and open pastureland. Just as he was about to ask what was going on, they rounded a curve and he saw a huge brick home that looked like something out of a Civil War movie. And up a hill past the house two buildings that looked almost like barracks surrounded by fencing. A big sign with Summerall Kennels painted in curly black letters on a white background stood next to an archway over the road leading up to the house and kennels.

"These folks must be rolling in money." He remarked to Ian

Ian glanced over at him. "More money than Croesus. And tight as a tick with it on top of that." He slowed the truck as they came even with the monstrous house.

"No." Gage said, listening to his instincts. "Go up to the kennels."

Ian cut his eyes over. "Are you sure? We might get on the wrong side of them if we go up there without one of them as escort."

"Ian. Trust me. I have this instinct that I've always listened to and never been sorry. If it turns out to be wrong this time, I'll take the blame."

After another moment, Ian pressed the accelerate, taking them past the house and up the hill.

As they rolled to a stop in a gravel area between the two buildings, a silver haired man exited one of the buildings, and with an angry look on his face, stomped toward them.

"Old man Summerall." Ian said.

But Gage had already figured that out. This man was the one ruling the roost.

Gage jumped out of the truck and met the man halfway.

"What do you think you're doing?" The man asked in a harsh voice. "The two of you are trespassing." He glanced past Gage. "You know better, Ian Elliott. You're from around here and you know we don't cotton to anyone just showing up snooping around out here."

Before Gage could reply, Ian stepped up beside him.

"Yes. Mr. Summerall, I do know how you

conduct business out here. But Holly Grace Hill is missing and we're out here to see if you've seen her. Or if anyone who works out here has seen her."

The silver haired man stomped up to them, putting a finger in Gage's chest. "Y'all get off my property. I haven't seen anyone who doesn't belong here."

Over the older man's shoulder, Gage saw a young woman exit the second building. A cacophony of dogs barking sounded before she shut the door cutting off the sound.

"What's going on out here, Grandpa?" She asked as she strolled over to their group.

Gage took in a deep breath, prepared to do whatever it took to get a tour of all the buildings. His instincts were singing so loud he was surprised the others couldn't hear it themselves.

Before he could speak, he heard a distant shout. He held up his hand silencing the surprised old man, and the not so surprised young woman. The distant sound came again. Like a woman shouting or screaming. Coming from the building the young woman had exited.

"I think you should take us through the building you just came out of." He said to the woman. "It sounds like there's someone in trouble."

She sniffed. "There's nothing going on. Sometimes the dogs sound like a human when they're behind walls like that."

Ian stepped up, locked eyes with Gage, sending a message Gage had no trouble understanding.

"Now, Mindy. I don't recall that those dogs have ever sounded like humans." Ian said to the woman. Her grandfather stood to the side with a puzzled look on his face.

Gage took full advantage of their focus on his friend and sprinted to the door of the building in question. Yanking the door open, he began shouting for Holly Grace. Which wasn't the best idea under the circumstances because the dogs housed in the building set up barking and howling so loud that he couldn't hear anything but them.

Scanning the building he saw it consisted of a center isle with cages on each side, ending in a door in the far wall. Sprinting, he made short work of the distance to the door.

He wrenched the deadbolt on the door and swung it open.

Holly Grace jumped into his arms. He swung her up and carried her out of the building to the gravel parking area.

The silver haired old man gaped at them while his granddaughter looked angry.

"What the hell, Mindy?" Ian asked angrily.

"She reported us to the authorities. Said we're running a puppy mill out here. I just wanted to scare her. I didn't hurt her at all."

"You're going to jail, Ms. Summerall. And I will personally see to it that you are prosecuted to the fullest extend the law allows. You just stay right where you are until the local law enforcement gets out here to officially arrest you."

Gage carried Holly Grace to the shade under a big oak tree and gently set her on her feet.

"Are you okay? She didn't hurt you?"

Holly Grace grimaced. "No, I'm fine. I'm just mad I couldn't get myself lose from that room. I had no idea who put me there, but I knew where I was as soon as I woke up." She rubbed her hand through her hair, trying to comb out tangle and winced.

Gage carefully probed her scalp and found a scrape. Holly Grace pulled away from his fingers.

"You've got a knot and a scrape on your head. She must have hit you with something and knocked you out after she lured you out there with a story about a rescue dog."

She melted into his arms and whispered. "Thank you for coming for me."

He pressed his lips to hers, leaned back and said, "I will always find you, love."

HANDLING HARLEY ANN

Susan Boles

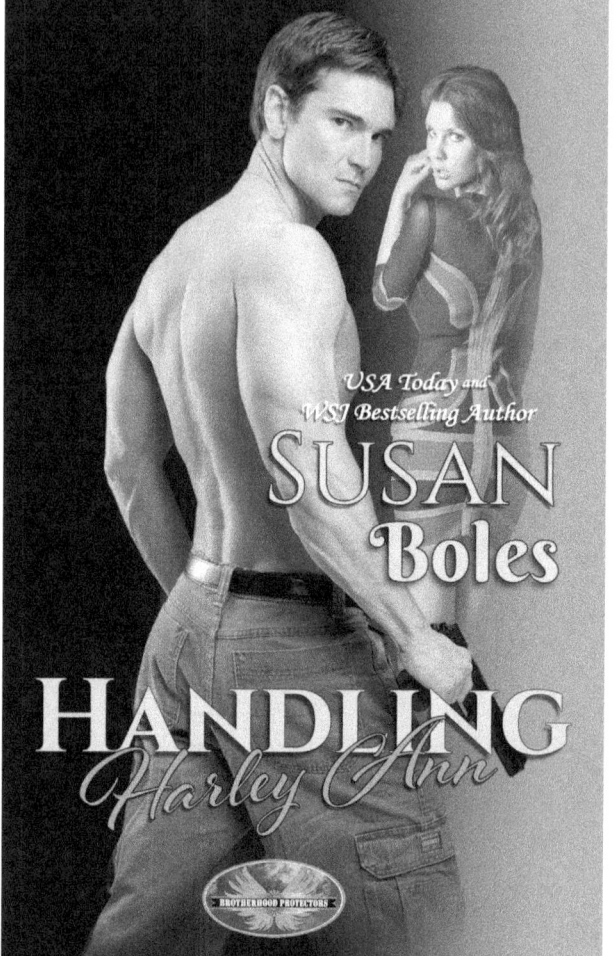

USA Today and
WSJ Bestselling Author

SUSAN
Boles

HANDLING
Harley Ann

BROTHERHOOD PROTECTORS

CHAPTER 1

"So, tell me how this town got a weird name like, Mercy." Jesse "Bird dog" Miller said as he sat back in the wicker chair on Ian "Hawkeye" Elliott's front porch in the town by that name. He'd arrived late last night on orders from Hank Patterson, their mutual Brotherhood Protectors boss in Eagle Rock, Montana.

"There are weird town names in Montana, too." Ian protested defensively.

"What? You mean like Eagle Rock? Eagle, as in the birds that live there. Rock, as in there are a lot of big boulders around because of them mountains. Perfect sense."

"I didn't mean Eagle Rock and you know it. I actually don't know how *this* town got its name. I'm sure it made sense to the people who settled here." Ian paused thoughtfully. "Lily Gayle Lambert would be the one to ask about that. She's the local genealogy expert. Among other things."

Jesse crooked an eyebrow. "What other things?"

Ian laughed. "She's the sheriff's cousin and she's always getting involved in his cases." Ian took a swig of his tea. "Drives Ben Carter bonkers. But what's he gonna do? Put his own cousin in jail?"

Jesse laughed. "Family! What can you do?"

Ian gave him a sharp look and he squirmed inwardly. He didn't have any family and didn't want any. From what he could see, family caused nothing but problems.

Ian went on as if he hadn't noticed Jesse's sudden silence.

"She's actually pretty good at figuring things out. The wolf man case was a real eye opener around here and the ripple effects are still going on."

"Come on." Jesse said, glad to move on to another subject. "A wolf man? No way. That's movie stuff."

Ian put his feet up on an ottoman and settled back in his chair. "Laugh if you will, my friend. But it's the truth. You can read all about it in the newspapers. Or ask Lily Gayle. Piper will introduce you. Lily Gayle is her 'courtesy' aunt."

Jesse shrugged. "I'm not that interested in looking it up. Or spending time chatting with someone old enough to be my mother who thinks she's a modern day Mata Hari. I'll take your word for it."

Ian shrugged. "Up to you."

"Aren't you wondering what brings me to your little burg?" Jesse inquired.

Ian raised an eyebrow. "I figure Hank sent you out here to find out what's the hold up on me coming back to Eagle Rock."

Jesse nodded. "You figure right."

Ian sighed. "Piper and I are still getting her daddy settled after him nearly getting killed a couple of months ago. The case that Hank himself sent me out here to handle."

Jesse eased back in his chair. "What was the deal with that? Wasn't it supposed to be a mob hit?"

Ian's eyes went dark. "Yes. There was a mob

hit out on him. He'd been giving passing information to the government about illegal deals going on in the state."

"Whew! Who knew so much intrigue went on in these sleepy little towns down south." Jesse sipped his own tea and went on. "I don't think Hank expected you to marry your assignment's daughter."

"Neither did I." Ian said. "But when we saw each other again. Spent some time together. Well, we just clicked back together."

Uneasy with the direction their discussion had taken, Jesse said. "Hank wants to know when you're coming back."

"And he couldn't take my word for it over the phone that things are a bit complicated on this end right now and I'll be back as soon as I get things situated here?"

Jesse sank lower in the comfortable chair, putting his own feet on a convenient ottoman. "Hey, man. Don't kill the messenger. I'm between assignments and thought I'd come down here and be Hank's eyes and ears on the scene." He gave Ian a roguish look. "And to introduce myself to some sweet southern belles while I'm here."

Ian laughed. "You're like all the rest. You think the women here are all sweetness and light because of the accent. But, I bet you'll find out while you're here that there's a very real reason for the iron fist in a velvet glove saying about them."

"Is that right? Well bring them on, brother. I'm ready for my first lesson."

Piper, Ian's wife, came up the front walk just then, frowning.

"Well, aren't the two of you a fine lazy pair?"

"Ian's been warning me about the dangers of southern belles." Jesse said just to see her reaction.

To Jesse's amusement, she shot her husband a dirty look. "Is that right?"

Ian flushed and sat up straighter in his chair.

"Just telling him not to be fooled by the accent. You ladies are some ferocious adversaries when you're pissed off."

Piper laughed. "That's right." Her eyes moved to Jesse. "You listen to old Ian here. He's had years of experience dealing with us."

They watched in silence as Piper continued into the house.

"She's got you well trained already." Jesse remarked.

"Yep." Ian said. "She sure does. And I don't regret it a bit. She's well worth any trouble."

"Hm." He responded. "If you say so. I thought you were some badass warrior dude. If you're not careful you gonna get your man card revoked."

Ian reached out and punched him in the arm. "No way. Never happen."

BROTHERHOOD PROTECTORS

ORIGINAL SERIES BY ELLE JAMES

Hot SEAL Hawaiian Nights (SEALs in Paradise)

ABOUT ELLE JAMES

ELLE JAMES also writing as MYLA JACKSON is a *New York Times* and *USA Today* Bestselling author of books including cowboys, intrigues and paranormal adventures that keep her readers on the edges of their seats. With over eighty works in a variety of sub-genres and lengths she has published with Harlequin, Samhain, Ellora's Cave, Kensington, Cleis Press, and Avon. When she's not at her computer, she's traveling, snow skiing, boating, or riding her ATV, dreaming up new stories. Learn more about Elle James at www.elle-james.com

Website | Facebook | Twitter | GoodReads | Newsletter | BookBub | Amazon

Follow Elle!
www.ellejames.com
ellejames@ellejames.com

facebook.com/ellejamesauthor

twitter.com/ElleJamesAuthor